Dedicated to the memory of
Desmond John FitzGerald 1921-2009
and
Iris Vera 'Betty' FitzGerald 1920-2009.

Published in 2009 by Pont Books, an imprint of
Gomer Press, Llandysul, Ceredigion, SA44 4JL

ISBN 978 1 84851 045 6
A CIP record for this title is available from the British Library.

This book is published with the financial support of the
Welsh Books Council.

Printed and bound in Wales at
Gomer Press, Llandysul, Ceredigion

Nelson to the Rescue

SIMON WESTON
in collaboration with David FitzGerald

Illustrated by
Jac Jones

P o n t

Nelson to the Rescue

Chapter One

Hello! There you are. I've met some of you before, haven't I? But just in case you're new around here, perhaps I'd better introduce myself. My name is Nelson, Nelson the 'orse . . . sorry h-h-h-horse. I got that wrong in my first book too! You'd think I'd have learned to pronounce my aitches properly by now, wouldn't you? Mammy was always so particular about it.

If you haven't been here before, welcome to my stable at the back of the St Mary Dairy in Pont-y-cary, a stable which I share with a couple of rats called Rhodri and Rhys . . . and a pigeon with no sense of direction. Next door lives Cardigan, the ex-racehorse. He's old and he sleeps a lot. In fact he doesn't do much else. To be honest with you, I think he's a bit out of touch!

Out in the yard, there are some newts in the pond and a frog in a bow tie who thinks he's a special agent. Oh, and a bunch of rugby-playing ducklings called the All Quacks. So . . . just a normal stable-yard really!

I was hoping that when I retired from pulling the last horse-drawn milk float in Wales, life would get easier, but there's never a dull moment at the St Mary Dairy. Let me tell you about what happened last Sunday evening.

I was sat here in my straw, minding my own business, when Rhodri and Rhys, the two ridiculous rats, appeared over the stable door. They plopped down beside me and by the looks on their faces I could tell they had been up to no good.

'Nelson . . . Nelson . . .' they squeaked. 'Mike the Milk is going to meet the Prince of Wales.'

Somehow that didn't surprise me. Mike the Milk, my owner, has met loads of people. In fact he has met half of Cardiff. He's met three members of the Welsh rugby team and Tom Jones, the singer. He's even met Ryan Giggs! He also says he met the wrestler Hulk Hogan once, although I still reckon that was Mrs Harris from the fruit and veg stall in the market – they have the same moustache!

Anyway, the rats were jumping about and making a heck of a noise. It was giving me a right headache. 'Isn't it exciting? Isn't it exciting?' they squeaked.

I scratched my ear with my hoof. Yes, very exciting – if it was true – but something didn't sound quite right. 'The Prince of Wales. Are you sure?' I said.

'We've seen the letter. It came from Buckingham Palace.'

'Letter!' I said. 'What letter?'

'It's on his kitchen table . . . under the cornflake box and the butter dish.'

I folded my hooves and looked them straight in the eye. 'Under the cornflake box and the butter dish . . . in the kitchen . . . behind the door that's always shut . . . to keep out nosey rats!'

'Yes,' said Rhys quietly.

'Just happen to fall open, did it?' I said.

They looked at each other and their whiskers drooped. They both went a little red in the face. Those two are the nosiest rats I know! They are always sticking their whiskers into places that whiskers shouldn't go.

'We didn't open the letter,' said Rhodri. 'We just saw that it had a crown on it and that the envelope said that it had come from one of his 'omes . . . We weren't being nosey!'

'H-h-homes,' I corrected him. 'You must pronounce the aitch.'

'Aha!' said Rhys, waving his paw at me. 'There was no aitch at the beginning! It said 'omes. I expect he has got lots of 'omes, being a prince.'

'And, being Prince Charles,' said Rhodri, 'if he doesn't want to use an aitch, he don't 'ave to.'

'He doesn't have to,' I corrected him.

'Well at least we agree on that,' said Rhodri.

I was getting a little confused and annoyed so I told them off. 'You two are the nosiest rats on this planet. You shouldn't poke around in other people's mail . . . and how do you know it was from Prince Charles anyway?'

'Because of the fridge,' said Rhys.

'Prince Charles has sent Mike a fridge?' I asked.

'No . . .' said Rhodri, 'and . . . we weren't being nosey . . . there is a note on Mike's fridge which says *Tuesday, Prince of Wales, MBE*. Anyone walking through the kitchen can read it.'

'MBE,' repeated Rhys. 'That sounds important, very important. What does MBE mean?'

'It means Member of the British Empire,' said a voice above my head and a small grey feather floated down from the rafters. Flight Lieutenant Pigeon fluttered down shortly after it. He saluted the rats. 'Pigeon, Flight Lieutenant 24556695, at your service.'

Rhodri looked at Rhys and sighed. 'Why does he always say that? He's lived here with us for months...we know he's Pigeon, Flight Lieutenant 24556695.'

'Shhhh,' I said. 'Don't be rude. It's just the way he was brought up in the military.'

'Always repeating himself?' muttered Rhys.

'He never stops,' said Rhodri.

I glared at them. 'Will you two be quiet! He does not keep repeating himself.'

'Member of the British Empire,' said Flight Lieutenant Pigeon.

I don't know why I bother really, but I let him finish.

He puffed out his chest and continued: 'Had 'em in the RAF, don't you know. Given to people who really deserve a medal.'

The rats blinked and looked very impressed. 'Wow! A medal!' they both said.

'Oh yes,' said Flight Lieutenant Pigeon. 'He'll get it at Buckingham Palace in Liverpool.'

'London,' I said. That pigeon's got no sense of direction.

By now Rhodri was scratching his head and he asked the question that was on the tip of my tongue. 'What has Mike got a medal for? Has he been brave?'

Flight Lieutenant Pigeon thought for a moment or two and then opened his beak. 'This sort of medal can be given to anyone who deserves it. Not just for brave things but for working hard, raising money for charity . . . or . . . or . . . delivering the milk for year after year . . . after year . . . after year!'

'He's repeating himself again,' said Rhodri.

Rhys giggled. 'Sitting on a cart behind Nelson's bum for years. That's brave!'

'I've told you before, it's the oats,' I said with as much dignity as I could muster. 'If Mike bought me better quality oats, there wouldn't be a problem. Cheap oats give me wind!'

'Is that what's causing climate change then?' said Rhodri. 'Oat cuisine?'

The rats roared with laughter and rolled around on the straw. I tried to ignore them and, anyway, something was still troubling me.

'I don't believe this!' I said. 'I'm sure you've got it wrong. Mike can't be meeting Prince Charles for an MBE and certainly not on Tuesday. The Bluebirds are at home to Plymouth Argyle on Tuesday night and he wouldn't miss that for anyone, not even the Prince of Wales.' Mike's loyalty to Cardiff's football team sometimes ruffles a few feathers, especially when Sir Francis and the All Quacks are in training for a big rugby match.

Rhodri and Rhys stopped sniggering and put their little paws on their hips. 'Right, come with us,' they said. 'If you don't believe us, come and look for yourself.'

Chapter Two

I knew I shouldn't have said yes, but a few minutes later I found myself gently undoing Mike's back door and tiptoeing into his kitchen . . . well, tip-hoofing!

As it was a Sunday, Mike was out at choir practice. Actually, I think he calls it Barbershop singing! I'm not sure what Barbershop is but it sounds good. I think he goes and gets his hair cut and they all sing at the same time . . . a sort of Hairy St Mary's Dairy Male Voice Choir.

Anyway, I must admit that the rats were right.

'Look,' said Rhodri, climbing onto the table and pointing to the fridge. 'There's the note. *Tuesday . . . Prince of Wales . . . MBE.*'

'And look,' said Rhys, scrabbling up beside his brother. 'There's the letter with the crown from one of his 'omes!'

I looked. It was all true apart from one little thing. 'That says OHMS not 'omes,' I said. 'OHMS stands for . . . stands for . . .'

'Ogwyn Harris, Milk, Saturday?' suggested Rhodri.

'The Prince of Wales is hardly likely to know the orders on Mike's milk round, is he?' I said. Really those rats get more ridiculous by the day.

Rhys looked innocent. 'But he's got a lot of stables at his 'omes, hasn't he? Perhaps it stands for Old Horses May Smell?'

'No! It stands for . . .'

'On Her Majesty's Service,' said a voice behind me.

Well, I nearly jumped out of my harness! I shot forward and knocked over the cornflakes, covering Rhys completely. Rhodri stepped back into the butter, slipped off the table and fell into the bin, which wobbled a bit and then toppled over. I tried to turn round but my bum knocked all the cups and mugs off the Welsh dresser, smashing them on the floor, which was already covered in cornflakes, butter, rubbish and rats.

That's the trouble with being a Shire Horse and not a show pony. Plenty of muscle in my shoulders and back end but I'm not exactly dainty. 'Built for pulling, not pirouetting,' Mammy used to say. Out in the yard that's a good thing, but inside the house . . .

I glanced over my shoulder, expecting to see Mike, but it was only James Pond, that crazy frog in the bow tie who lives in the reeds on the duck pond in the yard.

'It stands for "On Her Majesty's Service",' he repeated from the doorway. 'Or in my case "On Her Majesty's *Secret* Service".'

'Do you have to go round frightening people like that?' I said. 'I thought you were Mike.'

'No, the name's Pond . . . James Pond . . . licensed to croak,' he said and hopped off.

I sat down with a crunch. Rhys had dug his way out of the cornflakes and Rhodri wandered past with a tea bag stuck to his head. I looked at the mess and folded my hooves. 'This is why I said that you shouldn't stick your whiskers into other people's business.'

Rhodri and Rhys looked at each other and shuffled their paws with embarrassment.

I stood up and crunched on some more cornflakes. 'We have got to clear this mess up . . . and now . . . before Mike comes back. And first thing tomorrow I have got to go and buy some new cups.'

The rats ran in all directions, picking up broken china and rubbish. At the same time, I was trying to sweep the cornflakes into a neat pile before sticking them into the bin, which was now the right way up. It took about half an hour to get the kitchen clean again and, shortly after that, I shut the door quietly and wandered back to my stable with the rats.

'Well I hope that has taught you a lesson,' I said, settling down on my straw. 'I don't know how I am going to tell Mike about the broken cups and why there are hoof prints in the butter!'

The rats giggled.

'It's not funny,' I said. 'Half of Mike's cornflakes are wedged under my hooves.'

Rhodri looked at my feet. 'Trod all over them, didn't you?' he said. 'Crushed them to death! Does that make you a cereal killer?'

Honestly, those two get worse every day. You should have heard the laughter. They laughed so loud they woke old Cardigan, who lives in the stable next door.

He looked over his door and yawned. 'What time is it?'

'Sunday,' I said. 'You know, the day you like to lie in . . . until Monday. You've got up a day early.'

'It was the noise,' he yawned. 'What's all the fuss?'

'Rats!'

'I was only asking,' he said.

'No . . . no . . . no! The rats have woken you up!' I tried to explain the situation to him. But after telling him about Prince Charles, the kitchen, London, the MBE and the broken cups, he just looked at me blankly.

It was Rhodri's question that seemed to bring him back to his senses. 'You've been to London, haven't you, Cardigan? I remember you told us once. You went to hide in a park. What's it like?'

'Hide in a park?' he said, looking confused. 'Hide in a . . . I went to Hyde Park! I have a cousin in the Royal Household, carries the drums and pulls the royal carriages, that sort of thing. *He* lives in Hyde Park. It's a very big place, London – a horse could get very lost, let alone a couple of rats.'

Rhodri and Rhys looked at each other and then back at Cardigan.

Cardigan narrowed his eyes and gave them a hard stare. 'You aren't going to London, are you?'

'No . . . no . . .' they said and scurried off into the stable-yard.

Cardigan looked at me and said, 'I don't trust those two.'

He was right. Neither did I!

It was getting late and I thought I'd better say goodnight to Cardigan as he was looking very sleepy. He had been up for nearly half an hour so I suggested he went back to bed for a bit of a rest.

I settled down and listened to Rhodri and Rhys laughing and whispering outside in the yard. I suspected there might be trouble the next day and I might just have to have a word with them. But it would have to wait. I fluffed up my straw and nodded off.

U

It was five o'clock in the morning when I heard 'Floatie', the milk float, starting up.

Mike popped his head over my stable door to say good morning. 'I might be back late,' he whispered. 'I've left you plenty of food, so see you later.'

I could hear the bottles rattling in the crates, and the purr of Floatie's motor disappearing into the early-morning air. Could Mike be sneaking off to London without telling me?

'Are you awake?' I said to the rats as I stretched and yawned and looked across to where they slept by the door.

But the straw was empty. Not a rat in sight! I got to my feet and looked out at the yard. Not a rat in sight there! I looked into Cardigan's stable. Not a rat in sight there either!

It was then that I realised what was happening . . . they had gone to London to see Mike get his MBE.

Chapter Three

At five past five, Sir Francis Drake and his rugby-playing ducklings, the All Quacks, jogged into the yard for their early-morning training.

'Sir Francis,' I said, 'have you seen the rats?'

He shook his beak. 'Nope! In training. Got a big match with Wasps at the weekend.'

For a moment I forgot Rhodri and Rhys. I couldn't believe my ears. 'You are playing "the" Wasps, the famous London team? From the premiership?'

'No,' said Sir Francis. 'Some wasps from the rubbish tip . . . about seventy, I think. Very good fly halves but no weight in the pack!'

'Look,' I said. 'I think Rhodri and Rhys have run away to London to see Mike get his MBE at Buckingham Palace tomorrow.'

Sir Francis looked at me and blinked. 'Have you been eating too many horse-and-pony nuts again?'

'No!' I protested. 'You know what those rats are like, one crazy idea after another. I'm afraid they have taken themselves off.'

'But how?' said Sir Francis.

I thought for a moment. He was right. How would they get to London? It came to me in a flash. 'By rail! Some while back Mike had to take his auntie to the station to catch the early-morning train. I was telling them about it. She thought it wouldn't be any extra bother for him because he'd have to meet the milk train anyway. Mike explained that milk goes by road tanker these days but he was still happy to give her a lift to the station. The train goes at about 4.30 a.m. That's the one they'll have caught, I bet, well Rhys and Rhodri at any rate.'

'Right,' said Sir Francis. 'Let's get to the station. We have to stop them! London is a dangerous place for two rats who don't know what they are doing. Just one question, which way is the station?'

'The station is just off James Street . . .'

I was interrupted by a voice. It was coming from the reeds lining the pond. 'Rats lost in London!' said the voice. 'This sounds like a mission for a special agent.' It was James Pond.

'Oh no! Not the crazy frog!' said Sir Francis.

'Look,' I said, trotting back to my stable. 'We need all the help we can get . . . even the frog.'

I pushed open my door. If we were going to London by train, we would need money for the tickets and I had a little saved for emergencies just like this one. Sir Francis followed me into my stable, with the potty frog close behind.

Flight Lieutenant Pigeon fluttered down from the rafters. 'What's happening?' he said.

'We are off to London,' said Sir Francis. 'You'd better come along; you might come in handy looking for Rhodri and Rhys.'

'London,' said the pigeon excitedly. 'I've never been to Scotland.'

I looked at Sir Francis. 'In what way is he going to be helpful?'

The pigeon was about to open his beak and ask about the rats' disappearance but I said I would tell him all about it on the train.

It took me a couple of minutes to find my money tin in the straw. Sir Francis helped me open it and together we rolled out the pound coins and five-pound notes.

'Wow!' said Sir Francis. 'Where did you get all this money?'

'Christmas tips mainly, and I have sold some things on the web,' I said.

'What, eBay?' said Sir Francis.

'No . . . Hay-Bay. It's a special site for horses. I've sold shoes and a horse collar and my stamp collection.'

'Well!' said Sir Francis and started to count the money. He took charge of the notes, with Flight Lieutenant Pigeon and James Pond holding the pound coins. We told the All Quacks not to wander off, and to go and wake Cardigan if there was any trouble. Then, we slipped out of the stable-yard and into the main street. It wasn't long before we came to the station and I could see that someone was just opening the ticket kiosk. We formed a queue at the window and waited for the shutter to go up.

'Good morning,' said a cheery voice from behind the glass. The voice belonged to my old friend Penny. She was sorting her tickets and hadn't looked up.

'Good morning,' I said. 'One horse, one duck, a pigeon and a frog. Return to Buckingham Palace, please.'

'Buckingham Palace? The train doesn't stop at Buckingham Pal...' Penny looked up and jumped. 'Nelson! Where are you going?'

'Buckingham Palace – to see if Rhodri and Rhys are there. And then, to bring them home.'

Penny looked a little confused so I tried to fill her in on the story so far. She listened patiently and began to shake her head. 'Those two rats are really naughty,' she said. 'Running off like that! You could be right; they might have caught the early train . . . it left at 4.30 but it's very slow. If you get the six o'clock, you should get into London just behind it. But you will

have to get from the station, through London, and then to Buckingham Palace by using a taxi or the Underground or . . . Are you quite sure you want to go to London?'

'We have to,' I told her. 'We can't leave those two on their own in the big city. How much for the tickets?'

Penny rang up the price on her till. 'It's very expensive!' she said.

'We've got the money, Penny,' said Sir Francis.

'Aah! Moneypenny,' sighed James Pond. 'Lovely woman to work with.'

'Oh no! You've set him off now. He thinks you're talking about James Bond,' said Flight Lieutenant Pigeon. 'Quick, get him onto the train; there's a queue building up.'

'Aah! Q . . . great man!' said James Pond.

I gave a big sigh. This was going to be a long day.

Penny smiled at me and whispered, 'The train leaves from platform "M" but I think you might want to keep that to yourself!' She was right. We didn't need any unnecessary delays. If James knew Penny was directing us to platform M, he'd probably think it was code for a meeting with the head of MI6. Someone once made the mistake of telling him that in real life the Secret Service supremo is known as C, not M. We all wished they hadn't! It caused confusion for weeks.

At five minutes to six, we all squeezed onto the train and settled back for the journey in Standard Class. Well, all except James Pond: he travelled by 'moist class', in the washbasin in the toilet, because frogs have to keep wet. Flight Lieutenant Pigeon perched on a handle which had a big sign above it saying EMERGENCY ONLY. DO NOT PULL! We thought it was a good idea to ask him to move. Sir Francis and I tried hard to relax. We both knew that looking for Rhodri and Rhys in London was going to be very difficult.

Chapter Four

Now, I don't know if you have ever tried to get a duck, a pigeon, a frog and a horse into a taxi . . . but take it from me: it's not easy. The trip to London seemed shorter than I expected and passed without too much fuss. There was one nasty moment when James Pond fell into the toilet bowl. He was a little flushed (and shaken) but not too stirred by his experience.

However, when we arrived at Paddington, there were crowds of people, there was lots of noise and it took ages to find a taxi with a sunroof.

I'm nearly seven feet tall and the only way I could travel by taxi was to stick my head out of the cab. That's why we needed a sunroof. The driver was a little surprised to see us but he said he knew where Buckingham Palace was, and off we went. There were people everywhere, with cars and buses and motorbikes but not one horse-drawn milk float in sight. Through the streets we drove until Flight Lieutenant Pigeon said that he had spotted a cousin of his in a place called Trafalgar Square.

'Look! Look!' he said. 'There's my cousin Monty!'

We all stared out of the taxi window at the hundreds of pigeons sitting in groups. There were pigeons on statues, pigeons on fountains, pigeons on tourists and pigeons on pigeons.

'Which one is he?' I asked, and instantly regretted it.

'Can you see the pigeon eating a hot dog and flapping his wings? My cousin is right next to him. He's the one with the grey feathers, and the shiny beak and the ring on his leg. He's sitting on top of a tourist, the one with the camera and the map, looking up at that . . . that thing!'

'That's Nelson's Column, mate!' said the taxi driver.

'Nelson's *column*?' I repeated. I craned my head upwards. There in the middle of the pigeons was a huge pole. Balanced on the top was the figure of a tiny milkman in a funny hat. I couldn't imagine why they'd put a milkman on top of a pole, though. And why did it have my name?

'What is Nelson's column?' I asked.

The taxi driver looked in his mirror and laughed. 'You ain't heard of Nelson?' he said. 'He was really famous . . . beat the French and saved England from a terrible defeat.'

'Oh, rugby player, was he?' I said. 'Sorry, I'm not good with the England team. He looks like a good fly half but he's a bit battered!'

For some reason Sir Francis tutted sharply and shook his head. I think I might have said something wrong but I didn't know that there was more than one famous Nelson. I had a Great-Uncle Nelson who pulled a brewery cart in Swansea, but he wasn't famous like me. Mind you, I have to say that the one standing on top of the pillar was the oddest-looking figure I have ever seen. He certainly wasn't related to me! What with only having two legs (and small ones at that), he wouldn't be much good for pulling milk floats!

After another ten minutes or so, the taxi stopped outside some railings and we all got out onto the pavement. Sir Francis paid the taxi driver and I turned round. What a sight! Wow and wow again! There was Buckingham Palace. I have never seen a stable like it. Heaven knows how much straw they get through in a week!

There were policemen on duty at the gates and, behind them, soldiers in red uniforms who looked as if they were wearing big black cats on their heads. There were hundreds of people on the pavement outside, people taking pictures, people getting into taxis, people getting off buses, people staring at Buckingham Palace . . . but there were no Welsh rats to be seen.

'Listen,' I said to the Rhodri and Rhys rescue team. 'I'll ask at the gates whether anyone has seen them.'

The policeman on guard duty was extremely helpful and listened to me really carefully.

'A couple of Welsh rats,' he repeated. 'No, I haven't seen anyone like that. And you say they are here for Mike the Milk and his MBE tomorrow?'

He pressed his radio and muttered a message. A muffled message was muttered back.

'Sorry,' he said. 'But I have checked with the office. There are no medal ceremonies for months, and nobody called Mike the Milk is on any guest list. I think you've got it wrong!'

My heart sank. Where were Rhodri and Rhys? What was I going to tell Sir Francis, James, and Flight Lieutenant Pigeon?

I was about to walk away when I heard a voice.

'I say!'

The policeman jumped. The voice had come from behind him.

'I say,' said the voice again. 'Is there any chance you could help me?'

The policeman stepped to one side and there stood a smartly dressed man in a suit. He was looking very worried.

To my surprise, the policeman stood briskly to attention and saluted him. All the soldiers in red (with the black cats on their heads) stood to attention too and saluted. When Flight Lieutenant Pigeon also sprang to attention and saluted, I just stood there, wondering who the smartly dressed man could be.

'Can you pull a carriage?' he said.

'Of course,' I said. 'How much milk has it got on it?'

'Milk! There's no milk,' he said, 'just me! One of my horses has got the flu.'

'Horse flu?' I asked.

'Horse flu,' he said.

'Bless you,' said the policeman.

'It would just be me in the carriage and I need a second horse to pull it,' said the smartly dressed gentleman.

'Oh, not a problem then,' I said. He wasn't very tall and I doubted if he weighed more than three crates of 'gold top' and a dozen yoghurts.

'Splendid,' he said, waving at one of the red-suited soldiers. 'I'll get someone to show you where the Royal Mews are. I expect you would like a wash and brush up.'

Well, by now I was totally puzzled. Royal Mews? What's mewing got to do with horses? Terrance – the horrible ginger moggy in Caitlin Avenue – mews every time Mike delivers the milk. I reckon it could mew for Wales!

Then it turns out that Mews is a posh word for stables. Nothing to do with cats at all. Luckily Lieutenant Pigeon – who has flown in some very grand company – managed to tell me before I made a real 'horse' of myself.

Anyway, before I knew it, I was hoof deep in fine straw, being washed from the tip of my nose to the end of my tail. Never in my life have I had such a make-over. Mike's really good about keeping my coat glossy. I get a regular grooming with the curry comb and dandy brush, and he takes great care of my hooves. Horse shampoo was new to me though – I thought I was going to pong like Mrs Rhys Davies after a session in the Pont-y-cary Beauty Parlour, but it wasn't too bad. Winning Streak shampoo turned out to smell pleasantly of new leather, though it lathered up rather a lot. I squinted through the foam to see if there was any sign of the well-dressed stranger. I could hear giggling from the top of the stable door. Through the soap bubbles I could just see the pigeon, the frog and the duck.

'You don't have any idea who that was, do you?' said Sir Francis.

I shook my head and bubbles shot everywhere.

'That was Prince Charles,' he said. 'That was the Prince of Wales!'

Chapter Five

Well, fancy me being in the Royal Mews at Buckingham Palace. The straw was softer, the water was clearer and the oats were sweeter than any I have ever tasted.

The company was a little strange, though, as standing in front of me were three small horses who seemed to be having a conversation with themselves.

'He's awfully big!' said one of them.

'I wonder what he's doing here?' said another.

'I've never seen one before, but I think he's a carthorse!'

A CARTHORSE . . . A CARTHORSE . . . I had to put a stop to that! 'Excuse me!' I said. 'I am a Shire Horse. My name is Nelson and I pulled the last horse-drawn milk float in Wales.'

All three just looked at me and blinked.

'So what do you do?' I asked, fixing them with one of my stares.

'We are His Royal Highness's Polo Ponies,' said one in a rather sniffy voice.

'Polo Ponies! There's fancy. Well at least I work for a living. I don't hang around all day eating mints!'

That showed them. One of them was about to say something back but James Pond jumped into the drinking water and started to splash.

There was a chuckle of laughter from the stable beside me and a voice said, 'Hello, Nelson. Cardigan said I should look out for you.'

I popped my head around the stable door and there stood a tall grey horse with broad shoulders and a long white flowing mane. He was huge, as big as me . . . and then some!

'Who are you?'

'Raglan. I'm Cardigan's cousin. He said you might be popping down here. He called me this morning on his mobile.'

My mouth fell open. I was amazed. 'Cardigan has a mobile phone?'

'Oh, yes. We are on the same package . . . Oats 2. Unlimited texts and a hooves-free headset. We talk most nights about all sorts of things: you, the yard and Mike!'

It was then that I remembered why we had come to London in the first place. All this fuss and attention had made me forget about Rhodri and Rhys.

'The rats,' I said out loud.

'Don't worry,' said Raglan. 'They are safe in the stable at Pont-y-cary.'

'They're what?' I exclaimed. I couldn't believe my ears.

Sir Francis, a dripping James Pond and Flight Lieutenant Pigeon all put their heads round the stable door to listen.

Raglan looked a little uneasy. 'Cardigan told me they wandered back to the yard about an hour after you left. They went to buy some replacement cups or something. Some idiot smashed a load belonging to Mike.'

I shuffled my hooves as Raglan continued, 'I'm afraid your trip to London has been a bit of a waste of time.'

I groaned. All this way and those two ridiculous rats were at home. I have told them time and time again that they must tell people where they are going if they want to wander off. And now I'd done exactly the same thing!

'Still!' said Raglan. 'You are helping me pull the Prince of Wales in his carriage this afternoon. We couldn't do it without you. It will all be over by four o'clock and we can have you back on the train and home in two shakes of a mare's tail.'

I arched my shoulders and relaxed a little. He was right. I was helping somebody. I was big enough to pull a carriage with Raglan. Let's face it, the Polo Ponies couldn't have done it. They were tiny. They probably had nice minty breath but they would not be very strong.

The time passed very quickly and by about one o'clock, I was looking my best. I was a shiny new horse; even my mane had been plaited and tied in ribbons. Sir Francis, James Pond and Flight Lieutenant Pigeon all tried not to laugh as I was taken out of the stable.

'You look like a movie star,' said Sir Francis. 'You know . . . thingy . . . what's the name . . . that Jones person.'

'Indiana Jones?' I said hopefully.

'No . . . Catherine Zeta Jones,' he said and they all laughed.

Raglan came and stood beside me. He was all polished and buffed and had his mane tied in the same way. 'Listen, it's a very important job we have to do, Nelson. Don't take any notice of them. We have to look our best and remember we're going to be on television.'

Television! Nobody had mentioned television. I looked at Sir Francis. 'I'm going on television,' I said.

'I know,' he said.

'Probably all over Great Britain,' I said.

'Probably all over the world,' he replied.

'Seen by millions of people,' I said.

'Yes . . . in ribbons!' he chortled.

Before I could say anything else, Raglan and I were placed in a big

harness and a huge golden coach was rolled up behind us. A man in a white wig and a long silver-and-red coat with knee-length trousers introduced himself as the coachman and suddenly my ribbons didn't look stupid at all. The coachman climbed on board and flicked the reins, and we were off.

'We'll wait here and watch it on TV,' said Sir Francis.

I shouted goodbye.

The coach wasn't that heavy. I have had heavier things to pull at Christmas on the milk round, like when Mike decided to deliver the turkeys for Merv the Meat, his mate from Merthyr. Merv's butcher's van had broken down so Mike the Milk had volunteered me to carry them. A cracking Christmas surprise that was!

Even when Prince Charles got in, dressed up in all his regalia, Raglan and I could still pull at a steady trot and soon we were passing through the gates of Buckingham Palace and out onto the streets of London. By now, four police horses had joined us and so had some of the soldiers in red with the big black cats. The Household Cavalry, according to Raglan, were right behind us and a band with a big drum marched in front. It was very noisy and I may have got the name wrong but I think Raglan called them the Ice Cream Guards.

'I won't forget this, Nelson,' said Prince Charles as he started waving to the crowd. 'It's very kind of you to help out.'

'Not a problem, butt,' I said and Raglan nudged me.

'You can't call him butt!' he whispered and he told me how to address the Prince of Wales properly.

I smiled over my shoulder and nodded: '*Dim problem*, Your Royal Harness.'

I am not sure, but he seemed impressed that I had got his name right.

Chapter Six

Now, I don't know if you have ever been to London, but I hadn't, and got quite a surprise! The streets are a bit bigger than in Pont-y-cary. There are also a lot more people and the whole population of London seemed to have turned out to see the Prince. Some were waving flags – and I was glad to see that there were some Welsh flags there – other people were taking pictures, and everyone seemed happy and smiling as we turned left at the top of the big road that leads away from the Palace and then right . . . and then left again . . . and then right. I was already lost!

'How do you know where to go?' I said to Raglan as we went round a roundabout.

'I have a computer screen just here,' he said, pointing to his collar. 'It's a special "on board" navigation system for horses called "Sat-nag". I just type in the address and it works out how to get there.'

I was really impressed. Raglan was using all the latest technology. He said he'd picked it up 'on the hoof' but I wasn't sure I believed him.

On and on we plodded until the Ice Cream Guards – well, that's what it sounded like when Raglan said who they were – suddenly stopped playing and we all came to a halt. The Prince of Wales got out of the coach and vanished into a big building.

'Now what?' I said to Raglan.

'We wait! He's only gone for lunch.'

'Lunch!' I said. 'It takes a hundred soldiers, a band, four policemen and a coach to take him for lunch. I bet that jams up the drive-through when he goes for a burger! And think of the money! You could probably feed a racehorse stable for a year on what this has cost!'

'Hush! It's a very special lunch,' said Raglan. 'It's a group of ladies from Pembroke and Carmarthen. They have come all the way down to tell him what's going on in their area. It's called the West Wales Women's Wealth, Health and Welfare Watchdog. They do lots of things to help the environment.'

'Good!' I approved of that.

'He'll only be an hour,' said Raglan. 'Unless he has to do a speech, that is. The West Wales Women's Wealth, Health and Welfare Watchdog is a bit of a mouthful. We could be here all afternoon.'

I looked at him nervously but he smiled back. 'I'm joking! We'll have you on the train to Pont-y-cary and back home in no time.'

Well, we waited and waited. People took pictures and I was about to ask Raglan if I could get an ice cream from the Guards when suddenly I noticed that a television camera was pointing at us and a lady with a microphone was coming towards me.

'Hello,' she said. 'I'm from BBC Wales. We understand you have saved the day for Prince Charles. Can you tell us all about it?'

I put on my best voice and remembered not to drop my aitches. 'Yes,' I said. 'My name is Nelson the h-h-h-horse. I h-h-h-have come down from the St Mary Dairy in Pont-y-cary to look for a couple of rats who ran away without telling me where they were going and I thought they were coming to see Mike the Milk get an MBE at Buckingham Palace. But it's not true. He's not getting an MBE, and the rats are still at home anyway. They only went to buy cups and mugs to replace the ones I smashed in Mike's kitchen because I thought Prince Charles had sent Mike a fridge. And then this other h-h-h-horse got ill with h-h-h-horse flu.'

'Horse flu?' she said.

'H-h-h-horse flu!' I repeated.

'Bless you,' she said.

'Thank you . . . and then His Royal Harness asked if I could pull a carriage and I said yes because he's not very heavy – about three crates of "gold top" and a dozen yoghurts – and now he's with the West Wales Women's Wealth, Health and Welfare Watchdog and my train goes at five!'

The lady from BBC Wales blinked.

'Was that OK?' I said. 'Are you going to put Welsh subtitles on it?'

'We might have to put English ones as well!' she said as she waved to the cameraman to stop filming. Then she pointed out a second camera crew. 'I think that my S4C colleagues are rather hoping that you'll do an interview for them too.'

'Oh, I don't know,' I said. 'I've been learning Welsh but I still make lots of mistakes . . .'

'I'm sure that won't matter,' she said. 'Just give it your best shot!'

And so I did. It was easier than I thought. And the interviewer was really kind. Just as he was saying thank you – *diolch yn fawr* – the band started up again and I could see Prince Charles walking down the steps of the big building and waving goodbye to the West Wales Women's Wealth, Health and Welfare Watchdog.

Back through the streets with the soldiers, the band and the police, back through the gates of Buckingham Palace and back to James Pond, Sir Francis and Flight Lieutenant Pigeon.

Prince Charles jumped down and came round to talk to me. 'Many thanks, Nelson!' he said. 'For your services today I am going to add your name to the book of VIPs.'

'Thank you,' I said. 'What are VIPs?'

'Very Important Ponies,' he said.

'But I'm a h-h-h-horse!'

'In that case I'll get you an entry in *Hooves Who*. It lists only the finest animals.'

Wow, *Hooves Who*. I had heard of that book. You have to be a really important horse to get into it. Winning racehorses, horses that have carried generals into battle and Black Beauty, they're all in *Hooves Who*.

'I expect you'll want to get home now,' said the Prince. 'Let me get you a police escort to take you to the railway station.'

'Police Escort!' I said. 'I don't think I could fit in an Escort; I had problems in that taxi. Have you got a h-h-h-horsebox?'

He smiled at me, and moments later all four of us were riding in the smartest horsebox I have ever seen. It even had a television, and there I was – on the news! Luckily the newsreader had only just started the introduction. 'Today in London, a Welsh carthorse saved the day for Prince Charles!'

CARTHORSE! . . . CARTHORSE!

Sir Francis, the frog and the pigeon fell about laughing and then my interview came onto the screen and the laughter got even worse. It only stopped when the screen switched to the next item, something boring about the House of Commons, though I couldn't see so much as a blade of grass! My friends up on Pont-y-cary Common would have something to say about that.

'Quick!' I said. 'Turn over to S4C and we can see my Welsh interview as well.'

'I'm afraid not,' said Sir Francis quickly. 'You'll just have to hope Cardigan's recorded it. I don't think the reception's good enough in this horsebox.'

I snorted in disgust. 'I thought that was the whole point of saddle-lite broadcasting, that you can get any programme anywhere, even in a horsebox in the middle of London. It's just as well that we're on our way home, isn't it!'

Chapter Seven

The sign for Pont-y-cary railway station arrived very quickly and we scrambled out onto the platform.

Penny came running up to meet us. 'Welcome back,' she said and threw her arms around my neck. 'Nice hair,' she said.

(I had forgotten to take the ribbons out.)

'The whole town is talking about you.'

'Did you see me on television?'

'Yes, but never mind . . . the whole of Pont-y-cary is very proud of you and we are glad that you're home safely. Come and see.'

As we walked out of the station we were met by a huge crowd of people waiting on the pavement. They all clapped and cheered, well all apart from Cardigan and Mike the Milk, who were standing right in the middle and, I must say, looking very unhappy.

'And where have you been?' said Mike in a stern voice.

'London!' I said. 'To rescue Rhodri and Rhys!'

Rhodri and Rhys stepped out from behind Mike. 'Sorry, Nelson,' they said together. 'We should have told you where we were going.'

'And you should have told me, Nelson,' said Mike with a sigh. 'But you are all home safely now, so let's go and have some tea . . . in my new cups.'

Later that evening we sat around Mike's table and drank tea and had crumpets and laver bread with butter and honey (well, not on the same crumpet of course!).

All except James Pond. He had crept in and was sitting in the sink with a plate of flies and some pondweed. He wasn't really allowed in the kitchen as Mike didn't like the little puddles he left.

I began to tell the story of our adventures in London and Mike started to chuckle. 'So, how did you get it into your mind that I was going to get an MBE?' he said.

'Because of the note on the fridge!' I said, pointing to it.

'And the letter with the crown on it,' said Rhys.

'The one from Prince Charles with 'omes on it,' said Rhodri.

'OHMS!' I corrected them. 'We worked out that stood for *On Her Majesty's Service.*'

Mike looked puzzled for a moment, then wandered over to the fridge and found the envelope the rats were talking about. Then he took down the note. 'Oh no!' he said. 'Tuesday . . . Prince of Wales . . . MBE.' His chuckle turned to a laugh. 'Crown and 'omes on it.' The tears of

laughter rolled down his face. 'Tuesday . . . Prince of Wales . . . MBE,' he repeated.

'What's wrong?' I said.

'The *On Her Majesty's Service* letter came from the tax office. It's a Government department. That's why it had a special logo. And tomorrow,' he said, settling himself down and pouring himself another cup of tea, 'tomorrow, Tuesday, I am going to the Prince of Wales pub in Caitlin Avenue. They have started ordering their milk from me and they want me to deliver butter and eggs as well. Milk, Butter, Eggs – MBE – that's how I reminded myself of the order. Don't you remember, Nelson? You were the one who showed me how to use a special memory system in the first place.'

Well, I bet you didn't know that horses can go red. Two rats went red as well. I couldn't see the frog as he was in the sink, and the pigeon and Sir Francis have feathers, but I bet they were as embarrassed as I was.

'Don't read other people's correspondence,' said Mike, glaring at Rhodri and Rhys. 'It can only lead to trouble.' He gave a big sigh and settled back. 'But not to worry. You're all safe now and I think you have all learnt a lesson. Let's get to bed as we've got a long day ahead of us tomorrow . . . starting at the Prince of Wales with milk, butter and eggs!'

I finished up the tea, and Rhodri and Rhys crammed the last of the laver bread into their mouths. Sir Francis and Flight Lieutenant Pigeon pecked up the remaining crumpet crumbs and James hopped out of the sink and slid under the table, hoping to escape Mike's notice.

'Let yourselves out and try not to smash anything!' said Mike, tidying up.

We all wandered back to the stable, where Cardigan was settling down for bed.

'I didn't know you had a mobile phone!' I said to him.

'I bet you didn't know I had a cousin either,' he yawned.

I suddenly jumped. 'How rude of me! I didn't even say goodbye.'

'Don't worry. Give him a call,' he said, handing me his phone. 'If he's not in, you can send him a "hay-mail" later on my computer.'

I was stunned . . . again. 'A *hay-mail*? You have a computer as well?'

'Of course! I may be old and a little sleepy but I am a modern horse at heart. I bought an Apple last month . . . and, as everyone knows, horses love apples!' He smiled.

Suddenly there was a crash from Mike's kitchen and the sound of china smashing. The kitchen door swung open and there stood Mike with a plate of flies and a handful of green slime.

'Who has left these disgusting things in my kitchen?' he shouted. 'There's pondweed in the sink!'

As a small splash came from the pond, I realised that life was back to normal at the St Mary Dairy in Pont-y-cary. It was great to be home.

Anyway, that's what happened to me. How's your week going?

Read more about Nelson and his friends
in the first story in the series,

A Nod from Nelson.

Nelson's got 'retirement'.
It's not an illness, just
something which
happens to old carthorses
at the end of their career.
But Nelson's boss, Mike
the Milk, has problems
with his new milk float,
and crossword expert
Nelson finds himself
called out of retirement
to head off an
environmental
disaster!